About the Author

Ray Dillard is a sixty-nine-year-old retired teacher and administrator. He attributes his understanding of the human spirit and its need for nourishment and growth to his experiences as a son, brother, husband, father, and teacher. *The Wichita Discovery* is his second book. He has published poetry and personal narratives in magazines and his work has often been used for oral reading competitions.

The Wichita Discovery

Ray Dillard

The Wichita Discovery

Vanguard Press

VANGUARD PAPERBACK

© Copyright 2024
Ray Dillard

The right of Ray Dillard to be identified as author of
this work has been asserted by him in accordance with the
Copyright, Designs and Patents Act 1988.

All Rights Reserved

No reproduction, copy or transmission of this publication
may be made without written permission.
No paragraph of this publication may be reproduced,
copied or transmitted save with the written permission of the
publisher, or in accordance with the provisions
of the Copyright Act 1956 (as amended).

Any person who commits any unauthorised act in relation to
this publication may be liable to criminal
prosecution and civil claims for damages.

A CIP catalogue record for this title is
available from the British Library.

ISBN 978 1 83794 088 2

This is a work of fiction. Names, characters, businesses, places, events and
incidents are either the product of the author's imagination or used in a
fictitious manner. Any resemblance to actual persons, living or dead, or actual
events is purely coincidental.

Vanguard Press is an imprint of
Pegasus Elliot Mackenzie Publishers Ltd.
www.pegasuspublishers.com

First Published in 2024

Vanguard Press
Sheraton House Castle Park
Cambridge England

Printed & Bound in Great Britain

For my family. Without their love and support, this story would not have been written.

A special thanks goes to my oldest granddaughter, Leila. Her art and encouragement served as motivation for this work. And, to my wife Vicki, who is my reason for everything.

1

We had planned to hike the Wichita for over a week. J.J. and I were only thirteen years old and thought we knew what we were doing. Little did we know that three miles as the bird flies was closer to fifteen if you followed the river. It was full of bends turning right and left. We hiked toward every point of the compass and down on the lower bank, you couldn't see where you were. The colossal cottonwood trees that lined the banks of the river compounded the fact that we were twenty feet below the upper bank. The giant trees had bloomed, and the female trees had produced bundles of fruit that looked like tiny grapes. They were beginning to rupture and would soon fill the air with tiny cotton puffs that carried their seed as far as the wind or water could take them. We didn't think to take water or snacks on the journey. John Junior and I couldn't have imagined what the day would hold. Or the next week for that matter. What we thought was a short hike, turned out to be an arduous trek that was physically challenging and filled with unbelievable discoveries.

Mom agreed to unload the two of us at the river bridge on the highway to town. From there we would hike the south bank and move upstream until we were close to home and could hike south to my house. We were just dumb kids that didn't know anything but excitement. We soon learned the river was full of mystery and had secrets of its own. We should have left some of those secrets buried in the river bank.

The river had returned to its normal trickle after it had been swollen from an early spring deluge. It was an ugly reddish-brown in color and had several places that could be easily crossed by foot. However, we kept to the south bank just as we planned. After about an hour and a half, we could hear faint music and murmurs of a distant conversation coming from the north bank.

"What's that?" asked J.J.

"I don't know," I replied in a hushed tone, tapping a finger over pursed lips, and adding a "shhh" for emphasis. We had hardly spoken since we left the bridge. We thought it might be fishermen trying to snag an early run of Sand Bass. As we approached, we could see they had no visible equipment for fishing but were camouflaged to hide their presence. Maybe they were moonshiners, or maybe they were operating a small clandestine drug lab. No matter which, we kept in the salt cedar and brush and moved quietly past. And two kids didn't want to deal with men that were hiding for any reason. We were about forty yards upstream when we were spotted.

"Hey! You kids! What are you doing snooping around here? Stop! Stop runnin!" His voice was thick with country and sounded mad. "Git back here!" I only had a quick look at him and had a flashback of an old movie and banjos playing. We were getting farther away when we heard a four-wheeler fire up and about four cranks of the throttle wind up the RPMs.

"He's a coming!" a frightened J.J. exclaimed. If he had looked back, he would have been scared for sure. The guy on the four-wheeler had a shotgun and was trying to cross the river. We were lucky though, as the water was just a little too deep and the small ATV drowned out and started to drift downstream. Another man on the bank standing by the camo tent fired a shotgun at us. I could hear it ripping through the new spring leaves and bouncing off the bark of the cottonwoods. It was like a shot falling downrange after a hunter shot at a dove.

"They're shooting at us!" a scared J.J. said with labored breath. "They're gonna kill us!"

"Keep running! I know what a shotgun sounds like. That's birdshot. Right now, they're trying to save the four-wheeler." The men were both trying to save the machine's slow movement with the river current. The brush and trees on the second step of the riverbank provided good cover but slowed our movement. I thought we were safe when I faintly heard one of them holler.

"I know who you are!"

"Do you know those guys?" J.J. asked, still running.

"Heck no! Not that I could tell."

But our community was small, and I represented the fourth generation to live there. For all I knew they might be waiting for me when I get home.

"Did you recognize either one of them?" I asked.

"You got a better look at them than I did." He was probably right.

"I don't think he knew us. He was using an old Carney trick. You know when you go to the carnival, and they claim to know Mary or Ann and ask if you know them. Just to get you to talk."

We continued dodging brushes and making tracks.

"I can hardly wait to tell everybody about this. Nobody's gonna believe what happened."

"We better keep this to ourselves. You don't know who they are. I got a pretty good look at them, and I don't know either. Maybe they had more business down here than us. Heck, they might even own the property and thought we were trespassing. We are trespassing, you know. Technically."

"Trespassing my rear end! We know just about every landowner upstream clean to the next county."

And he was right.

2

We continued to move upstream. Always watching where we stepped and glancing back just in case they had followed us. We were really just young fishermen at heart and tried to stay close to the river so we could find a good-looking spot where we might return to fish. The lower bank along the river was made up of long sand bars that were filled with tracks of all kinds of game imaginable. I was studying a branch the size of a man's arm that had been cut down and stripped clean by a beaver when J.J. interrupted my trance.

"DANG! You need to come see this." He was looking down at the sand and pointing at a track. When I got close enough, I could see what had his attention.

"That's the biggest cat track I've ever seen." It was bigger than a circle made putting my thumbs and fingertips together. "Would you look at the size of those tracks. I've heard farmers and pumpers talk about a cougar roaming loose on the river, but this is the closest I've been to him."

"Slick," he said in a weak tone as he stared at the track. "I think this scares me more than those guys did. Why, that cat could be anywhere just waiting for us to stumble across him." And he looked around like he was gonna see him.

"That track's probably two or three days old." I tried to ease the fear a little. "You're right. Two days ago, we were miles from here. Chances are he's miles away." Maybe I was trying to convince myself. I noticed a little shake in my voice and hoped he couldn't tell. "Let's move back up to the top level and try to see where we are," I suggested.

"You darn right. I've been lost since before we saw those two guys."

When we left the second level, we had to cross a fence at the edge of the upper bank. It was about four feet straight up and the fence was perilously close to the edge. The ideal point to move up was about ten feet from the best place to cross. So, one behind the other, we climbed the little ledge and grabbed the barbed wire moving one hand over the other just like running a trot line. Then about the time we reached the crossing point, the grass beneath the fence exploded in our faces! We had busted a covey of quail that had about forty birds. I guess it was too early to pair up and nest. It seemed like they came up in a launching order, like little missiles or fireworks on the fourth of July. I managed to hold on to the next lowest wire with one hand and J.J. had two wrapped around the bottom wire and his feet were dangling as he fought for a new foothold in the bank.

"Dang!" That was J.J.'s favorite word. He used it a lot. "That scared me to death. My heart's pounding ninety miles an hour!"

I was going to say something much worse, but instead replied, "Me too! One of them hit me in the face."

We took turns parting the wire for each other to slip through the fence and shared comments about our location.

"Can you tell where we are?" I asked, holding my opinion for last.

"I don't have the slightest idea." Which is what I expected him to say. Then he asked, "Where are we? Can you tell?" He continued to study the terrain hoping to see something he recognized.

"Well," I paused as I assessed the area. It wasn't exactly like being lost on the highway or in town. We were in a pasture with lots of mesquite and knee-high weeds. I sure didn't want to walk out from here. There were no roads, and I was afraid of rattlesnakes. If one of us got bit here, we wouldn't be able to get help for sure. By moving my view point a bit, I could see a radio tower. "I know where that tower is. But we need to go back down the river to get there.

"Why's that?" He quizzed me.

"Well, we won't have to cross any fences down there. And we might find a really good fishing hole that's closer to home. Besides, not as many snakes."

"Are you sure about that?"

"Have you seen any yet?" Not that we would have seen them anyway. You could step on one and that's the only way you would know he was there.

"Okay," he said as he headed back to the fence.

3

Once again, we parted the fence and slid down the face between the second and third levels of the river bottom and made our way back to the river. We were both a little more comfortable now. There was no sign of campers, big cats, or exploding coveys of quail. We began to talk about anything and everything under the sun. We remained very aware of our surroundings.

"Slick," he began with an inquisitive tone, "how does a guy named Glen Moore end up being called Slick, anyway?"

"You mean you don't know?"

"Now why do you think I'd ask if I already knew?"

"Well, when I was six years old, my aunt Maggie gave me a burr haircut. I looked like a skinned onion." I waited for J.J. to stop laughing before finishing the story. "Dad took one look at me and called me 'Slick.' I guess it stuck. Nobody ever calls me Glen anymore, except for Mom when she's mad."

"I have heard that before." He raised his brow and nodded his head. And I knew he had.

"What'cha gonna draw for your art assignment?" he asked.

"I don't know. I haven't decided yet. I was hoping something from this hike would jump out at me."

"You mean like those quail?" He laughed and gave me a nudge. I noticed we were staying closer than before.

"Maybe. I think I'd get tired of drawing quail if I was to draw that many of them. Maybe I'll draw just one. I got a pretty close look at one." I rubbed my head as he chuckled.

"I'm gonna draw a big cat track. It'll be full size so everybody will feel scared like we were. Ya' think It'll scare everybody?"

"Probably not. They'll say it's just a blown-up drawing of your old calico cat's footprint."

"No way! Really?"

"I might draw a picture of a four-wheeler or a shotgun," I said.

"That might be too revealing. Remember what you said. We're not telling anybody about that."

"A pump shotgun might be easier to draw than some toothless guy with whiskers and his green cap turned backward."

"Whoa, now! You got a better look than you said." He paused and gave me a stare.

"That's the only thing I remember, honest. I didn't pick up any features that I could draw," I tried to reassure him. "Maybe I'll draw a barbed wire fence with a lone Bob White sitting on the top wire."

"That's more like it. Maybe we should draw portraits of the pretty girls in our class," he suggested.

"She might not be pretty by the time you finish drawing her. She'll take one look and git pissed and never talk to you again." I challenged his artistic skills.

"Well, she might like it better than a drawing of a shotgun."

"She?" I questioned. "You got the sweets for somebody special?" I asked.

"Maybe." And he paused. "What's it to ya'?" he asked.

"I've seen you making eyes at Annie." Antoinette was a French student that had been attending our school this semester. She would be going home at the end of June. All the boys liked her. So did all the girls. But my answer would need to wait.

"Listen," I implored. And then very quietly added, "Do you hear that?" And then answered just in case he didn't know, "It's a gobbler, and he's getting close." I clucked back at him using my mouth and the web of my hand. It didn't sound quite right, but it got his attention. He came from behind some brush and put on a show, puffing out his feathers and fanning his tail. His beard almost dragged the ground. He looked like a shooting gallery target moving from side to side strutting his stuff for a hen. Then, tucked his feathers and opened his wings to gather air and with about five flaps he soared across the river to the north bank.

"Man, that wa—" I held my hand to his mouth and cut the sentence short. I could hear something moving in the brush farther upstream and deeper in the brush. J.J.'s eyes were big as half a dollar as he could hear it, too. At first, we didn't know whether it was hunters or the big cat. I was just hoping it wasn't the men from the camo tent. As the sound came closer it became apparent that it was more turkeys. It was a group of gobblers that didn't have mates. Toms and jakes that came to the bank and flew across two and three at a time. They were pretty, and they were loud. "Dang! That was awesome! Eight, I counted eight." J.J. was really pumped. He had never been that close to the big birds before.

"They're neat, aren't they?" I asked as if I needed an answer. The big birds were pretty. They were worth the trip even if we didn't find a good place to fish.

We took time out for a restroom break. We'd been on the river for almost five hours. It was after two o'clock and we were thirsty and hungry. The biggest discoveries of the day were just ahead. After about an hour of walking through the brush, salt cedars and over the sand bars we found something unexpected. A small school of minnows was swimming just off the point of the sand bar. They made a dark pool that looked like a shadow moving just beneath the red water.

"Hey, J.J," I said softly, but loud enough for him to hear. "Look at this school of minnows."

"Man, that's the first real sign of fish we've seen all day." He was moving closer when a big sandie busted the top of the water and gathered a bite of minnows. It happened as I was trying to get a closer look at the river minnows. The big fish was a surprise, and I staggered a step to my right as I reacted to the unexpected splash. Surprise indeed! That seemed to be the theme of the day. It was quicksand! I got my right foot in the soft spot. It didn't take long to sink up to mid-calf.

"Help me, J.J.!" He was already on the ball. He had a broken limb about the size of a cane pole and six or eight feet long. I was about to sink my left foot as well. I was pushing against the sand and could find no grip to pull myself out. He offered me the limb which I gladly accepted and promptly broke. "Get me that big chunk of driftwood."

"What, pray tell, are you going to do with that? It's too heavy for me to hold out."

"Please, just bring it over here! Okay?" As he struggled to bring the larger lifeline, I watched the little fishes regroup and move safely around the jutting sand. From my perspective, they looked much safer than me. The quicksand was swallowing me just as the sandie swallowed the minnow. Same thing, just more slowly.

"Here's the big limb. Now what?" He couldn't see that I needed it for leverage.

"This stuff isn't like the quicksand in a Tarzan movie. Just get it close enough for me to lean on with my left arm and come over here and grab my right hand."

"No way! If I get stuck in that pit of sand, we'll both die!" There was fear in his voice, and he took another step back. He didn't notice I'd already begun to sink more slowly as I was finding a bottom to the hungry sand.

"J.J., do you see this chunk of driftwood sinking any?" It was on more substantial sand than my right leg. I gave him just a moment to study for himself. "Now come over here and take my hand and put a foot on this log. I've got to try and save my right shoe. There's no way I can make it back without both shoes." J.J. found the courage to help and moved close enough for me to grab his hand. With both of us pushing against the driftwood and a mean grip of our right hands, I was set free. My sneaker was intact.

"Dang, Slick." Like I said. Dang was his word. "I thought you was a goner for sure."

"Thanks a bunch!" What do you say to a guy that just saved your life? "We need to be more careful, walking out on the sand bars like that." That statement was just for me because I was pretty sure he wasn't going to walk away from the solid bank. Even if he was a hero.

4

We continued upstream toward a small rapid that had a basin on the other side. It made a whispering sound as the current passed through and left foaming eddies in the river's downstream edge. The pool formed by the rocks held enough water for swimming. We didn't swim though. We were distracted by a cool freshwater spring that tumbled and burbled as it fell from one layer of sandstone to the next ending in a pool about the size of a pickup bed. It was about ten inches deep and dropped out the distal end and continued across a stoned pathway as it talked its way into the river.

"Dang! Have you ever seen anything like this before?" an amazed J.J. questioned, not really looking for an answer.

"Look how these stones fit together. That's not by accident. Nature didn't do it." They were fitted like a master craftsman had been hired for the job. "I don't know how long these stones have been here, but somebody with tools and skills did this long ago. You see, there's not any mortar joining them together. It was a skillful job. And it was likely a major gathering place for the local population. Maybe Wichita Indians had a village right here."

"It's something to see all right. But all that clear water reminds me of how thirsty I am." We hiked on the river for six hours with nothing but dirty river water that we wouldn't drink for anything. I was thirsty, too.

"Do you think we'd die if we just got a little sip?" Why would I ask J.J.? "I'll sip a little if you will." I dared him to take a drink that might possibly make us both sick.

"Okay." He accepted my challenge. We both got on our knees at the edge of the collecting pool. We cupped our hands together and filled them with the cold water from the spring. At first, we sipped, then we gulped. And then we drank until we'd had our fill.

"Have you ever had anything so refreshing in your life. I think that's the best water I ever had." And it was good.

"That's better than an Orange Crush." J.J. was smiling from ear to ear.

We hardly had time to discuss our good fortune when we could hear the brush parting and branches popping. And then, the biggest dog in the whole county was staring us in the face. We were only scared because of the sudden appearance of the gentle giant of the canine species. Chasity was a rather large Great Dane. She was brown in color and looked like a littermate to Marmaduke. She came up to me and licked my face. Then, she did the same to J.J.

"I almost lost my water," said an excited J.J. "I thought about that big cat and nearly wet down both legs."

"She's a good sign. It means we're close to home! Her old home is about half a mile from the house. Her owners moved off and left her. Almost everybody feeds her, and she never goes without. Just look at her. She's become a community project."

"She's a pretty dog all right. So why doesn't somebody take her home?"

"A couple of people tried, and she keeps jumping out and coming back. She's like a homing pigeon. Always going back home. Besides, it's cheaper this way. You get the dog and only pay part of the bill."

"What about all her shots?" he questioned. "She could get rabies or something and die or have to be put down."

"Just lucky, I guess. I'm sure she hasn't been to the vet since she was a pup. She'd come closer to getting shot than getting rabies." She was lapping up a drink from the collecting pool. It probably wasn't the first time.

"Why would anybody want to shoot her?" He began petting her on the back. "That just ain't right."

"Well, there are mean people in this world. Remember when that kid from Wichita shot old Pepper's buffalo?"

"Like the guy that shot at us when we started this hike?" He made a fair comparison.

"Besides," I said, "who wants to have the responsibility of owning her if she bites somebody's arm off?" His brow was down, and his eyes were pinched into little slits.

"Do you think she'd do something like that? I mean, as sweet as she is."

"You never know. She kills coyotes sometimes, and drags their bodies home, like a trophy." I could tell he didn't believe me.

"She can't kill a coyote," he firmly stated. "Well, she's big. But a coyote? Coyotes are mean!"

"I've seen their bodies. She stacks 'em up like cars in a parking lot. Kind of like a personal toy box or trophy case. A coyote hunter told Dad that he was parked in a wheat field near here one night, spotlighting, and tried to call up a coyote. After about the third try he started to stick the spotlight out the window and before he could turn it on, Chasity jumped up and put her big paws in the window and slobbered down his door panel. He almost had a heart attack!"

"Dang!" Again. "I think I'd give up hunting."

"I'm sure seeing her in the window like that made him reconsider his pastime."

"She likes almost everybody, but she has a favorite," I stated an observation.

"Yeah, you!" he exclaimed.

"No," I chuckled. "She likes old Bushy," I told him.

"The guy who runs barefoot on the side of the road with his rifle?"

"Yeah, and most of the time no shirt."

"Hey, that's a scary guy." His eyes were big, and he was slowly shaking his head "no" and leaning back a little. Then I heard him take a slow shaking breath and audibly exhale just as slow.

"He's really kind of nice, once you get to know him. He's just a loner, like Chasity here." I continued to pet the big-hearted dog. "They're both selective about their friends."

"Is he your friend?" J.J. wanted to know.

"He's friends with Dad. Dad helped Bushy and his mom get set up after their house burned down a few years back. He gathered donation items like furniture and clothing and set the two of them up in a different place. Just like Chasity, everybody's got to have somewhere to call home."

"Bushy," he puzzled, "is that a nickname like Slick?"

"No, that's his name. At least part of it. His mom was Indian, and his birth name is Bushy-Top-Pine Todd. Everybody calls him Bush except his best friends. They call him Bushy."

"How did an Indian with a name like that end up here at Cook's Corner?" he asked.

"Mr. Todd moved here with his wife when Bushy was a baby. He grew up here and came home to make a living in the oil field. 'Ol Bushy went into the service right out high school and won a bunch of medals. He was like special forces or something like that. He signed up for a fourth tour and they sent him home."

"Wow, I guess he earned a trip home as a reward for his service."

"I think it was cause he was tired. He needed time for his body and mind to rest and get back to normal. Then, his mom had cancer and died. That was all ten years ago.

He's been running the roads ever since. Summer or winter, rain or shine, usually barefooted. Sometimes he wears sandals made from tires."

J.J. didn't have a chance to respond. I used Chasity as a crutch and helped myself off my knees where I'd been drinking from the pool. It was then that I made a discovery. "What's this? Look!"

"What is it?" He could see me scratching at the ground beside the stones that surrounded the pool. "Let me see! Is that an arrowhead?" I finally gouged it out with the blade of my knife.

"I think so. It's not perfect, but you can tell it's an arrowhead." It was about as broad as a quarter at the widest part of the base and tapered to a point. It was almost red and looked like a delta wing jet with little tail wings. It was just less than two Inches long and no more than a quarter inch thick.

"Dang!" he said again. "How come I never find anything like that?"

"For one thing, we haven't been looking for them." I continued to clean the keepsake in the water of the pool. "If it hadn't been right under me, I wouldn't have found it."

"Let me hold it, Slick." He was begging more than asking.

"Okay. Here you go," I said as I handed it to him. He admired the treasure, turning it over in his hand several times. "It's a beauty," he surmised. "I gotta find one of these for myself." He started to scratch at the ground with a stick and I stopped him.

"Wait, I think the best chance will be down where this spring meets the river. Follow me." Together we trailed the water of the spring to the river's edge, with Chasity by our side.

At first, we just gazed at the mingling of the clear spring water with the dirty water of the river. Then, I had an idea. "Let's pan the rocks in the bottom of the stream. Like we were gold miners." I cupped my hands together like I did when I was drinking from the spring pool. I used them like a tiny excavator bucket to gather a sample of rock shards from the water. Then held them in the clear running water of the spring and washed them clean. J.J. followed my example.

"Like this?" he asked, as he copied my actions.

"I guess. There's no right way I reckon. Just dip, clean, and look." I emptied my hands beside the running water and spread the rocks for inspection. J.J. did the same. After only a few tries, we had success. We each had five Arrowheads. Three of them were in perfect condition.

5

The time had come to leave the river. I had hoped Chasity would show us the way, but as we emerged from the bank above the spring, I could see the radio tower to the south. It was a communication tower for the largest well servicing company in the Cook's Corner area. I knew exactly where we were. "Let's head for that tower," I said with authority. "Don't fall in that gully." Stating the obvious. There was a trench cut in the earth about as wide as a doorway and twenty yards long. It was about six feet deep at the end where it emptied into the river and only one foot at the leading edge. It curved like a snake making its way to the river. It was like a crack in the earth spilling water and rich red riverbed soil into the Wichita. I called to J.J., "Come on. They're gonna be looking for us." But he continued to gaze into the abyss. "COME ON!" I said louder. But couldn't break him away. I went back to him and said, "If a fella was to fall in there, nobody would ever find him." Now we were both looking into the fissure when I saw what held J.J. captive.

"What the Dicken's?" I stared at our discovery. We both did. Bones! The skeletal remains of a person were imbedded in the side of the gully. We just looked at our find for a good while. We had both seen the dead before. But they just looked like they were sleeping. That was bad enough. This was different.

"I guess you're going to tell me we gotta keep this a secret, too," J.J. said.

"Nope," I said. "We've gotta tell. This is too big to keep secret. Who is it and are there more? Heck fire! There could be more under our feet."

J.J. looked at his feet and backed up a step as if he stepped into something and had to clean his shoes. He finally awoke from the initial trance. "Dang!"

"I want to get a closer look."

"No way!" he shouted. "I don't think it's a good idea to disturb the dead. "We don't need a ghost following us home. We've already got two guys that shot at us and said they know where we live. Ain't that menacing enough?"

And the thought had crossed my mind that the dead shouldn't be disturbed. I wasn't super religious but didn't relish the thought of some kid playing with my bones someday. "I'm not gonna bother anything. I just need to get a better look, you know. So, I can describe what we found. And I told you those guys didn't know who we were. So, ease up and let me study."

I went to the beginning of the gully and carefully made my way to the remains, being careful not to step on anything obvious. It was the remains of an adult, I thought. The bones of the one visible arm were long, and the even longer bones of the lower right leg were in the bottom of the cracked gravesite. The skull was mostly covered.

Much to J.J.'s disapproval, I took my pocketknife and scratched around the skull.

"Don't do that," he said through clinched teeth. "You're disturbing the dead and if that's not enough, you're gonna git both of us in trouble."

The dense soil at the bottom of the canyon had enough clay to form small blocks that lifted away from the skull. And then I saw the eyes. They were covered with coins that filled the sockets and were held in place by sinew that refused to give in to time.

From above I heard J.J. "Dang!" He was now lying on his belly and peering at the remains. "Are those Kennedy half-dollars?"

"Nope." I clearly didn't know what the coins were, but they were like nothing I had ever seen.

6

We left the gully gravesite and headed toward the tower. Chasity was at our side. We spoke about the skeleton and wondered who it could be. Was it a farmer, a rancher, or maybe even an Indian? I thought probably not any of those. The old coins that covered the eyes held the answer. They were tarnished and looked like silver. Silver coins that filled the eye sockets. There were endless possibilities. But the coins and their apparent age meant that it was a very old guy. Or, at least, a very old skeleton.

After we crossed the field, we ran down a dirt and gravel road used by oil field pumpers. Chasity ran point ahead of us until she stopped and smelled the road. She growled and barked her disapproval. We slowed down and approached with caution and could see marks made by a very large rattler that had crossed the road before us. He must have been as large as a man's arm. His trail had the effect of a train crossing with cross arms and flashing red lights bringing us to a stop. Then we hopped over it like it was a curse, you know, like 'step on a crack and break your mother's back.'

"Was that a—" he began to ask.

"Yep. And he was a big one." And just look at that. As my eyes followed the path of the snake, I could see why the trail was so wide. Two very large rattlers were mating in the clearing off the road tracks. They spiraled into the air about sixteen inches, twisted like two lengths of wire in a switchbox. It was only the second time I had seen such a thing. But I knew they were still paired up in early June. If you saw one, you better look for another. Or perhaps, a third, as the two large snakes could be males in a wrestling match trying to prove themselves for a nearby female. It's a winner take all match. They wouldn't bite each other, but if you bothered them, you'd find out how poisonous they were.

Before I had a chance to remind him to watch his step, he was running down the road behind Chasity. I heard a very low "Dang" as I worked to catch up.

"Take a left where the roads meet," I called out. "She knows the way."

The two of them made a small dust cloud of the fine dirt in the shallow wheel ruts that settled quickly. I ran to catch them keeping my eyes open the whole time. I felt a burst of energy and should have been tired after the long trek on the river. Maybe it was a second wind like the coach had always told us. Whatever it was, we both felt it. Track season is over. Maybe we were just in really good shape. But we didn't run like this at the district track meet. We stopped at the pavement and looked across the grass hayfield at my home. Only a half mile to go. We looked both ways before crossing and could see Bushy running on the left side of the road. There was an old yellow Ford pickup moving past him and the two passengers were shouting out the driver's window. He never even looked at them. But I did. The passenger was leaning across the truck to shout at Bushy. He wore a green cap and had a rough growth of whiskers. When he turned and saw us, he hollered and pointed. It was the guy from the river camp who tried to cross the river in the four-wheeler. And it was on a small trailer behind the truck.

J.J. spotted them at the same time. "I think that's the guys from the river!" he exclaimed.

"Run! Run across the hay field! Run for your life!"

"Try to catch 'um, Red. Git over there and cut 'um off." He was trying to stick a shotgun out the window in front of the driver.

"Stop, Danny!" He grabbed the gun and pushed it up. "What are you thinking? You can't go around shooting people." Red tried to reason with his younger partner. Then during the altercation, the truck ran off the road and a reflector hit the rearview mirror on the passenger side. Red over-corrected and the trailer whipped to the right blowing out a tire and dumping the four-wheeler which wasn't secured.

Danny craned his neck around in time to see his four-wheeler tumble into an upright position. He could immediately see the handlebars were bent out of shape.

"Dammit, Red! Look what those kids have gone and done to my ride. That's two times today."

Red had the pickup stopped and was getting out as he replied, "Danny, that was all your fault. You're always overreacting. Stop and think every once in a while. Why don't ya'?"

"Just look at my ride!" He was still upset and very loud.

Meanwhile, Bushy had caught up with the Ford and heard the conversation. He was carrying an old 30 caliber carbine just like always. He detoured to the right of the truck and stopped at the four-wheeler.

"What are you looking at you damn Injun?" Danny said. Red's words had fallen on deaf ears, and Bushy just moved his eyes from the four-wheeler to Danny.

Bushy just harked up a big green lunger and spat it on the seat of the ATV. "Maybe that will help you shine it up." And then he laughed really low while staring into Danny's eyes. Red held Danny back. He wanted to get the shotgun, but Red stopped him. Bushy continued down the road without a second thought. He was ready to handle anything those two could dish out.

Red then spoke through clinched teeth, "What did I say about taking time to think now and then?" He turned Danny to face him and said, "He would have killed you before you got the gun clear of the door!"

"Maybe you're right. But Red, one of these days I'm gonna git me a piece of that Injun boy.

Luckily, they had a spare tire and were ready to roll in fifteen minutes. They tossed the broken mirror into the bed of the truck and glared at the house where the boys had long been inside. Now, Red was sure who they were. At least one of them was W.C. Moore's son. And he knew where to find him.

7

She was glad to see the boys make it home. It was getting late in the day, and she thought they would have been home sooner. "I didn't think you were ever coming home."

"But Mom—"

She kept on talking. "I thought you were hurt, or lost, or maybe snake bit." She continued to hug them both with tears of joy flowing from her eyes. "I should have never let you go. I knew better."

"But Mom." She was finally listening. "The river's so crooked and bent. Why, I'll bet we walked twenty miles? We found—" and he was again interrupted.

"Aren't you boys hungry? I know you didn't take a thing with you." She was trying to take care of their hunger and all they could think of was telling her about their adventure. They didn't even ask for a drink of water. They were still energized by the spring water.

Then J.J. dug in his pocket and dumped the arrowheads on the table. They made a clatter. "Look at what we found, Mrs. Moore."

"Oh my!" she exclaimed. "You found some arrowheads."

Slick was fishing the arrowheads out of his pocket when he heard W.C. drive up. "Let's show my dad." They both ran out to the truck to show W.C. the arrowheads. He didn't even know they had been on the river.

"Dad, Dad!" They both raced to show W.C. what they had found. They were in such a hurry that J.J. dropped a very nice complete arrowhead and booted it toward W.C. He could see they were bringing something to him and saw the arrowhead as it flew into the air and came to rest at his feet. He bent his long body to the ground, picked it up, and held it in his very large hand.

"This is really nice, J.J.," he said while studying the find. "Where'd you find it?"

"We have a bunch of 'um. Enough to start a collection, Mr. Moore."

"What part of the river did they come from?" he asked like he knew they had been on the river.

After a short pause, Slick asked, "How'd you know they came from the river?"

"Son, did you forget? I've told you that I was a walking encyclopedia. I know everything, except where on the river you found them."

"Well," he began, "we found them at a spring that feeds into the river about a mile from here."

"I know the place," he shared, like the walking encyclopedia he claimed to be. "I used to catch sandies where the fresh water ran into the river. I'd catch so many I could hardly carry 'um out."

"How come you never took me fishing down there? It would have saved us a lot of walkin'."

"And, it would have cheated you out of a great adventure."

The boys were spreading the arrowheads out on the hood of the truck. Sorting them first by color, then by size. "We found something else on the river, Dad."

"What was it? A beaver dam?" And he smiled like he knew what they'd seen.

"Nope!" Slick answered with a smile on his face. Like he was writing a new page in the encyclopedia. Except nobody ever used the encyclopedia anymore. Not since Google came into play.

"Okay, what else did you find?" he asked like it couldn't be as good as a beaver dam.

"We found a skeleton!" And he waited to judge the impact on the self-proclaimed walking encyclopedia.

"What? A skeleton? Like a dead cow's bones?"

"No, Dad, this was a human skeleton."

"Are you sure?"

"Yep, a human skeleton," Slick proclaimed with authority as J.J. nodded in agreement.

"We'll have to call the authorities." He jumped into parent mode with meteoric speed, digging his phone out of his pocket like a gunslinger in an old western.

"Wait, Dad! There's more!"

"I've got to call this in. Somebody might have dumped a body and the Sherriff needs to know." Slick tried to tell him about the coins.

"Tell him it's a very old gravesite," Slick interjected.

"Okay, how do you know that?" Something else he didn't know. Slick was on a roll.

"Well," he drew it out for effect. "There were two very old coins over the eyes."

"Coins? What kind of coins?"

"I don't know what kind they were. The side we could see had a shield with different pictures in each corner. I think they're silver."

"What kind of pictures?" he asked, glancing from one boy to the other trying to get a feel for what they'd found.

"That's all I know. That, and they're big. Bigger than a Kennedy Half-Dollar but not as round. You know, like they were imperfect. And Dad if I'd only had a cellphone I could have taken a picture." He was using the opportunity to bargain for a phone.

"We'll take that up after dinner. Right now, I need to talk to the Sherriff's department. It looks like Sunday morning's going to be really busy."

8

Mrs. Moore prepared chicken fried steak for dinner. It was one of her specialties and she served it with cream gravy, black eyed peas, and cornbread. Nobody would go hungry at her table. And the hike was a good topic for conversation. That is, when anybody had an empty mouth and could talk. Except for J.J. He often spoke with his mouth full. Sometimes he had his foot in his mouth. W.C. was eating jalapeno peppers with his peas and cornbread like they were candy. They were hot and big beads of sweat formed on his forehead and rivered down his brow to the bridge of his nose. He would dab the sweat with a napkin now and then to keep it from falling from the end of his nose. Slick's two younger brothers were eating like there wouldn't be enough or maybe like it was their last meal. The two little ones were always within reach of W.C.'s long arms while at the table in case they got choked or needed correction. They were aware of his presence at all times.

J.J. managed a few words past his cornbread and gravy. "You sure are lucky, Slick." He managed to swallow. "I wish my mama could cook like yours." And he reloaded with a fork of chicken fried steak.

Slick answered as soon as his mouth was empty. "Yep, Dad picked a good one. But I think it was cause she was so pretty." He winked at his mom, and she smiled back at him.

"Sounds like you boys had quite a day." W.C. was ready to start up a conversation about their hike on the river. "You found arrowheads, the spring and the skeletal remains of some pioneer I guess."

Before Slick could say anything, J.J. began to speak, "While we were at the spring, we were surprised by Miss Chasity." His eyes were big.

W.C. chuckled. "I bet that was a helluva surprise. Did you wet your pants?"

"No, sir, but nearly. It wouldn't have been so bad if we hadn't seen that big cat's footprints earlier. I was kind of aware after that."

W.C. rose up from a mostly emptied plate of food to look at the boys. "You say you saw tracks?"

"Yes, sir," he continued before Slick could say a word. "They were this big." He showed W.C. a circle he made with both hands. "I'm going to draw one for the end of the year art project. I'm sure glad we saw Chasity and not that big cat!"

"That cat probably saw ya'll, though." He was again exchanging looks from one boy to the other.

"You don't have to scare the boys like that, W.C.," Ellen said to her husband. "They'll be afraid to go back, and you know they want to go fishing!"

"They'll be okay. They're more likely to die from thirst than being mauled by a cat," W.C. said.

The boys looked at each other and Slick couldn't stop J.J. from talking. "We weren't going to starve with that spring water to drink. It sure was good."

"Tell me you didn't drink from that spring," W.C. implored.

"Dad, we were thirsty or else we wouldn't have."

"You boys will probably both have the trots or worse maybe." He looked at Slick. "I've warned you about drinking from the river or the canal. People might have dumped raw sewage in the river. You don't know what's in the river water."

J.J. looked at Slick. "Is the trots what I think it is?"

"Diarrhea," Slick affirmed his deduction. The look on his face indicated how bad it might be.

"If you get the belly ache, you better head to the restroom," W.C. said. "For all we know it was spring water that killed that guy whose remains you found."

"Or he might have been shot," J.J. said to offer another possibility. Slick gave him a hard stare so that he remembered not to tell about the men from the river.

After an awkward pause, J.J. said, "Don't worry, Slick, I wasn't gonna tell about those two guys." And, just like that, the cat was out of the bag.

"Yeah, Slick. You tell us about the two guys," demanded W.C.

The rule Slick had long adopted was to tell the truth. Sometimes though, he didn't tell the whole story. More so where his mom was concerned. But he didn't dare tell a lie to his dad.

"Well." He took a long, slow breath and audibly exhaled slowly. He was thinking. "We saw two guys on the river. I think they were on Keith's place."

"That's a good guess, seeing how he has about 2500 acres on the north side of the river. How come you didn't already mention that you saw two fishermen?" He was trying to get more information out of the boys.

"Um." He took another breath. "I'm not so sure they were fishing."

"Well, what did they say they were doing?

"We didn't talk to them," Slick said while staring a hole into J.J.'s eyes. "We were trying to mind our own business.

"Didn't they see you?" he asked. There was an odd moment while the boys looked at each other and W.C. and Ellen looked at them. Their eyes moved from one then to the other.

Then J.J. broke the silence. "Slick, I wasn't going to tell W.C. about that guy shooting at us with a shotgun." He thought for just a second and very softly muttered, "Dang."

"They shot at you?" he asked. "With a shotgun!"

"One guy shot over our heads to get our attention, but we just kept on running." Slick told him.

"The other guy tried to cross the river on his four-wheeler but couldn't make it," J.J. added.

"Who were they, Slick? Did you know them?" W.C. asked them both.

"No, sir. I've never seen them before," Slick answered.

"But we did see 'em again. On the way here." J.J. couldn't wait to point it out.

W.C. turned his full attention to Slick, shifting his weight in the recliner to lean toward Slick. "So." W.C. paused and looked at Slick as if he had been withholding information. "J.J. says you saw them again." Again, he paused. "Is that so?"

"Yeah. Down at the curve when we crossed the highway headed home. They were driving by in an old Ford pickup with a trailer hauling that four-wheeler. I think it came off the trailer and Bushy stopped to help them. But I don't think they wanted his help."

Danny and Red spent the last two hours before nightfall repairing the four-wheeler. They had to get the river water out of the fuel delivery system and tried without much luck to straighten the handlebars.

"Danny," Red said with one last grunt. "I think that's the best we can do." It was still apparent that it had been in a wreck. "If it won't work, we'll look for a replacement in town or online."

"Thanks for your help, Red," Danny said as he inspected Red's work. "Let's crank her and see how she runs."

"Go ahead and crank it up!" It took a few tries, but it finally started.

"You're a genius, Red!" he said as he gunned the engine a few times.

"Take it easy, Danny! Why is everything always wide open with you?"

"It sounds great, Red." And he gunned it two more times. Red put one hand on Danny's throttle hand and gave him the cut motion at his throat with the other.

"It's late. We better whup up some grub and get some shut eye."

"Okay, Red. I'll go warm it up."

"Please, no TV dinners tonight. Open up a can of beans and we'll eat the last of the cornbread. Tomorrow we'll get up early and clean up the camp. I don't want those boys to bring W.C. to look around."

This time, Danny jumped to follow Red's orders. Too bad he didn't always do that.

W.C. finally got the sheriff on the phone, and they planned to meet at the house at 8:00 in the morning. That meant no church for me. I would be the guide and the sheriff wanted to hear my story. We took J.J. home and Dad relayed our story to his parents. They were visibly shaken but glad we were both safe. I'm quite sure their eyes bulged when they heard J.J. tell his version. I could hardly wait till Monday morning. I wanted to hear what he had to say and see what he had drawn for his final art project. And I wondered how he would react to mine.

9

Dad was up earlier than usual on Sunday morning to make his rounds. He had responsibilities that must be taken care of, and they trumped meeting with the Sheriff. Everything had to be going up and down in the oil patch and both oil and salt water must be going together and separately to determined locations. He used a bright spotlight and the light of the skyline to check every location. The spotlight served him well to spot varmints that would fall to his rifle. Although he surely did, I never saw him miss. While he rarely saw traffic on early Sunday mornings, he did meet a ford pickup with bright headlights two miles west of town. He couldn't follow them because of time constraints, and they would surely notice him making a turnabout.

When he returned home, he woke us all and started breakfast. It was a Sunday morning ritual. Mom would take care of herself and get the little guys dressed for church. He made what he called bachelor's breakfast: fried bacon, added to finely cubed potatoes that were stir-fried until they started to brown and finally combined with a half dozen eggs. We didn't have a toaster. It was my job to make cinnamon toast. Buttered bread was covered completely with a sugar and cinnamon mixture and placed in the pre-heated oven. And when I say completely, I mean to the crust. The boys wouldn't eat it if it wasn't completely covered. Breakfast was ready in 30 minutes time, and we gathered to eat with the boys leading the table prayer. It might sound like Mom had the morning off, but it was a much greater challenge to dress the boys and then dress herself. She looked like a movie star when she entered the room. Dad met her with a kiss and got the chair for her just like we were in a fancy restaurant. Her coffee was poured and ready.

The Sheriff arrived at 8:01. He was dressed in his daily uniform. He wore a short sleeve khaki shirt that had two pockets and pants that were a darker shade of khaki. All were pressed and you could see his white undershirt between the unbuttoned shirt collars. He stood almost six feet tall and was short compared to W.C. While he was broad at the shoulders, he appeared more rotund through the mid-section. I attribute most of his girth to his bullet proof vest. He wore a gun belt and taser with handcuffs and ammo pouches loaded with clips for his pistol. He wore field boots and a 7-point star placed above his left pocket, which along with his tightly groomed speckled grey goatee, gave him the look of authority. He was barely out of his vehicle when he greeted Dad. "Good morning W.C."

"Good morning, Bob. You had your breakfast yet?"

He nodded yes. "I stopped at the Driller on the way here. That's the best place on a Sunday morning. It wasn't too crowded, and the service was good."

"Do you need another cup?"

"No, I've got a thermos in the unit." He nodded to the car seat. "Are you ready to get started?"

"This is Slick. He'll show us where to go."

"Okay, Slick. Lead the way."

Dad and I climbed in his truck and headed to the river with the Sheriff close behind.

We turned off the highway and never saw a soul. That doesn't mean no one saw us. Around the curve and down the road a beat-up yellow Ford pickup saw us turn off the roadway.

"Are you seeing what I'm seeing?"

"That's W.C. ahead of the Sheriff, I think."

"We better turn around and go the back way. The last thing we want is for the Sheriff to stop us. And who knows what those nosey kids told him," he told Danny.

"Now, Red, you said they couldn't see what we were doing."

"They probably couldn't, but we scared the hell out of 'em and I shot over their heads. It might be hard to convince anybody that I wasn't tryin' to kill 'em."

"I still want to kill 'em!"

"That's another good reason not to talk to 'em. Your temper and a pickup loaded with this drug making stuff."

And with that they turned around. Once again keeping their secret safe.

It took two trips to move the lab supplies to the shed behind the trailer house.

We were soon on the two-track road, and I pointed in the direction of the gulley.

"Yup, that's the way I remember."

We left the little road and soon approached the gulley. Dad stopped the truck and I quickly bailed out.

"Wait a minute," the Sheriff called out. "Let me catch up and we'll go together."

I led them both to the gulley at exactly the right spot and we peered over the edge together. "There it is. Not like it was going anywhere." How astute.

Bob went to the shallow end and squeezed his way down to the remains where he began to study the find. "This is an old gravesite." Studying the skull he said, "I'll bet it's over a hundred years old. Those old coins will probably help date the remains."

After a short pause, I responded, "I figured that and I'm only thirteen." That might have sounded a little smart because it caused me to get a sharp thumb in the back. "Well, Dad, I'm pretty sure those are Spanish dollars, or what they call 8 Reals. Anybody that had Mr. Smith for World History would know that."

Dad responded long and slow, "You didn't say that last night." The walking encyclopedia was faltering.

"Well, the light's better this morning and I can see for sure. I saw them in my history book last night. A long, long time ago they were really common." My response sounded a little too bright. "I mean, they were used for centuries as money around the world. There's no telling how long he's been dead."

"One thing for sure," Bob replied. "The coroner's gonna want to look at this, and the State and Federal Indian authorities will want a look, just to make sure it's not Indian remains. That would string this out for a long time." And, then he added as he was working his way back to the top, "I'm gonna flag and tape this off. I don't want anymore human traffic in here." He looked up at me. "That means you, too, Slick."

"Can I get a picture for a keepsake? I mean I did discover it. Along with J.J., that is."

Bob couldn't resist my pleading and after a short moment replied, "I guess that would be okay. But I'll do it. Just give me your phone and I'll snap a few shots."

Turning to Dad I held out my hand. He was already holding his phone out with the camera ready. Bob re-entered the trench and snapped a few shots of the remains. Then did the same with his phone. "I should have done this already. Thanks for the reminder kid." And when he was done, he slithered out and went about the job of marking the site. He threw red flags like darts into the ground and drove lath stakes to hold a yellow crime scene ribbon like you see on television. It looked like he'd done it before.

"This place belongs to Mitchell Hobbs, doesn't it?" he asked Dad.

"Yeah. Old Mitch won't get too stirred up by this. Unless there's money involved."

"I don't think there's gonna be any money, but there'll be some traffic in here. That might not please him much. I'll let him know."

"There's one more thing, Bob. When the boys were on the river, they ran across two campers that were staked out under camo."

"Yeah?"

"They shot at the boys for no reason."

"That's pretty serious. Were you boys giving 'um any trouble?"

"No, sir! We were just going our own way, looking for a good fishing hole," I told him.

"They tried to talk to us, but we started running. That's when the guy shot up in the trees. He said he knew who we were. I didn't know him, though. And we just ran for our lives."

"A chocolate bar would have been a better way to get your attention than a shotgun, don't you think?" And he chuckled just a little.

And Dad said, "I don't see much humor in being shot at, Bob."

"I know. I'm sorry." Seeing his mistake. "Can you tell me anything about 'um?"

"Outside of needing a shave and wearing a green cap I don't know much. We did see them later, though. They were in a beat-up yellow Ford pickup." And I retold the story just as I had for Dad. That included seeing Bushy talk to 'um.

Then Dad said, "If you don't find these guys before I do, I'll take care of it myself."

"Now, W. C., this is a matter for the law. I'll file an incident report for the remains and the shooting. I'll get a Deputy on it first thing Monday morning and I'll keep you in the loop. Promise."

We left the riverside ravine and headed our separate ways making dust clouds from the dirt roads that rose into the sky and mixed with the cottonwood seeds that were beginning to fall to the earth.

10

At home again, I studied the pictures of the remains. Along with my history book, I began to draw a picture of the skull with Spanish Dollars covering the eyes. The skull was like an x-ray shown bright on a black background with the silver coins shining like lights from the eyes. Broken and missing teeth added to the eerie appearance. The shading of the crown and facial features made it scary for sure. It was like the man's spirit was alive on the page.

I also started another drawing. I tried to capture Annie with a colored pencil drawing. I didn't need a picture to draw her. I had made a mental note of her features in art class. Her smile, the color of her hair and brow and the way her hair flowed to the top of her shoulders and bounced as she moved about the room. I tried to catch her brown eyes and the way light would twinkle in them as if it burned from within her soul. And that look that they had when she caught me looking at her. It was mysterious and alluring. She would be gone in a week, and this would be my going away present. I hoped she would like it.

It was bedtime when I finished, and I was tired after a long day. Mom came into the room and checked out my art and said it was spooky and romantic. Then she laughed and said she wouldn't say which was spookier. She was seeing her oldest beginning to grow into an adult. I guess that's scary for any parent.

Bright and early Monday morning, a greenhorn deputy was parked off the roadway on the north side of the river bridge. Buster was young and inexperienced. He wore a cap with the sheriff's insignia that had a flat bill like the young baseball players wore. His uniform wasn't neatly pressed like Bob's and the shirt and trousers were of the same brand but had stains from the snuff he had drooled from the oversized three-finger dips he was never without. He frequently wiped his mouth with his bare hand and then rubbed his hands on his pant leg. He didn't need to dress as neatly as Bob, he thought, because he was not an elected official. Bob tried to explain the connection between his appearance and the office of County Sheriff, but it didn't get through to him. His uncle is a county commissioner and has a strong influence on Bob's office. As a result, a wet behind the ears twenty-two-year-old was seemingly being groomed for the office of sheriff.

    He often missed calls on the radio because he had it turned down to sing along with the local country station. And many times, he would remove his bullet proof vest and throw it in the passenger seat, because he deemed it uncomfortable and unnecessary. Besides, what was Bob gonna do? What could he do? His uncle would threaten to reduce funding and cut numbers. He felt secure.

Today he would see no sign of the two suspects. They were working on an oilfield rig that was headed to another county.

11

At school, Slick and J.J. shared their adventure story with teachers and classmates. J.J. was a colorful storyteller and took advantage of every opportunity to embellish the experiences we had shared. He certainly had Annie's attention. She clung to every word.

"We narrowly escaped the clutches of death from the hands of deadly criminals!" he told them. "Slick was sinkin' to his waist in quicksand, and I had to save him from sure death! He wouldn't be here if it wasn't for me pulling him free." He went on and on. I did have to agree with his description of the covey rise, however. It was even more explosive and sudden than he described.

"And then we found these arrowheads," as he displayed them on his desk. "While we were looking for more of them, a big dog the size of a lion burst through the tall grass and scared us both half to death." He held his hand up to show Chasity's size. He didn't get to talk about the discovery of the skeleton. Mr. Smith, who also taught art, was trying to gain control and begin class.

"That's all very interesting, J.J. If I could have your attention, we've a lot to cover today. It's the last day of art class and I'm anxious to see what you've prepared for your final project. Now, if you would, please clear your desk of everything except your drawing tablets and open them up to your drawings. I hope you're all prepared, as this is a very important grade."

We all scurried to follow his directions and he walked the aisle monitoring our progress. We were soon ready, and he stopped at each desk to see what we had produced, commenting and showing each to the class. We reacted with applause and verbal approval and maybe some laughter if it was appropriate. Mr. Smith was very complimentary to everyone. He chuckled when he saw the big cat track that J.J. had presented.

"Whoa! What have we here? You've drawn a very large cat track." And then, just as I had predicted, he said, "Is that from your family pet?"

"No sir!" J.J. exclaimed. "That's the drawing of a cat track we saw on the river Saturday."

Then he looked at me for confirmation.

"That's right, Mr. Smith. It was every bit that big." I backed him up.

"See?" replied a vindicated J.J. "We could have been killed and eaten at any moment."

There were oohs and aahs from the class.

"Well, I can see the reason for your concern. Thank you for sharing your experience with the class." Then he caught a glimpse of my drawing across the aisle. "Well, Mr. Moore. What have you dreamed up for us? It's certainly intriguing. Are those pieces of eight covering the eyes?"

"Yes, sir," I responded.

"That's a very nice likeness of old Spanish coins. And that skull is almost ready to come to life!" he said as he smiled and continued to gaze. "Whatever gave you this idea?"

"Well, while we were exploring the river, we found a skeleton embedded in the wall of a gully. There were Spanish dollars covering the eyes. I just thought it was interesting. You know, you don't see that every day."

Several members of the class, including Annie, were trying to see the drawing and he held it up and panned it from side to side. Then, as he showed the picture around, another picture slipped from the folder and landed on the floor between me and J.J. It was the colored pencil sketch of Annie. Time kind of froze for just a minute. Four sets of eyes stared at the portrait: Mine, J.J.'s, Annie's and Mr. Smith's.

"Would you look at this?" and his jaw dropped as he bent down and retrieved the art. "This is a tremendous replica of one of our classmates. You have captured Annie perfectly. She looked so real she could begin to speak. Just look, Annie. What do you think of this?"

I knew I was beginning to blush. It wasn't my intent for the portrait to be presented to the class. There were a few oohs and aahs and one "oh my." In the back, one said, "That's really good, Slick."

Then again, he asked, "What do you think, Annie?"

"I think he's wonderful." And I saw it in her eyes. That same warmth and connection I had felt before. I wasn't blushing anymore. It was a different warmth than I had felt before. And it was welcome.

Across the aisle, I saw J.J. take a page from his art folder and wad it up. There was steam building, and he was red and didn't look at me. Dad always said, 'nothing caused trouble like girls and money.'

Mr. Smith asked to speak to me after class. As I approached, he asked, "Do you realize the significance of your finding the skeleton?"

"I know it's got a lot of people hopping. The sheriff, the coroner, Indian Tribal officials, and I think, historians are going to be the most interested."

"That's what I'm thinking. The dates on those coins are going to rewrite the history of our region. Don't you wonder who he was and what he was looking for?"

"He was just an explorer looking for riches. Probably lost and alone and all he found was hunger and death."

"Your pretty astute for a young man. And you're probably right. It'll be interesting to see what comes from it."

I answered with an uncharacteristic, "Yep."

And he added, "Your drawings were really good today. I hope you continue to pursue something with that gift you have."

"Thanks, Mr. Smith. I just hope It doesn't cause me any trouble." And I turned to walk out the door.

J.J. was waiting outside. "You're no friend of mine! You dang back-stabber!" And he punched me in the left eye. It was a pretty good jolt, and my books started sliding from my hands. After I got them under control, I raised my hand to feel my eye. It was gonna be a shiner for sure. That's when I saw Annie coming from the ladies' room. She saw the whole thing. I know I didn't look like much of a man, but she didn't seem to care.

"Let me see." She raised my face with her left hand under my chin and softly rubbed under my eye with her right. "Oh, my goodness. Wait here and I'll be right back." She dashed into the ladies' room and came back with a moistened paper towel. She placed it over my eye saying, "Now hold it there for a few minutes. There's no need to hurry to math class. We're just going to turn in the books and play number games, anyway."

"Annie," I began, "I wasn't going to show the drawing to the whole class. I was going to give it to you as a going away present. Then it fell on the floor, and you see what happened next."

"It's a very nice portrait! And I'm quite flattered. I'm flattered that you even drew it."

I sat my books down and took the portrait from my folder. "Here, this is for you." It was signed and dated.

"Thank you so much, Slick. I will treasure it forever as a memory of my visit." Then she kissed her finger and placed it on my eye. "Come now, let's move to class."

We walked the now empty hallway to math class. I carried my books in my right arm and she held my left hand. It was the best black eye I ever had, and it didn't hurt at all!

12

W.C. was on his way back to the shop from the supply store when he spotted Bushy jogging down the highway. He pulled over before they met and got out the dice. You see, they would always roll high dice for a dollar whenever they met. They broke about even, and it wasn't because either one of them was trying to make money. It was just a friendly game, and it was always for a dollar. Sometimes they rolled double or nothing after the first roll and it never went past that. It was just a chance for W.C. to check in on a friend, and he was proud of the job the local boy had done serving our country. W.C. drug his lanky frame out of the truck, shaking the dice in his right hand. "Are you ready to lose a dollar?" And he laughed really big and smiled.

"We'll see who loses a dollar. I believe it's your turn to roll first, ain't it?" Bushy always remembered whose turn it was.

W.C. rolled the dice on the hood of his truck, and they stopped on a five and a three. "Eight!" he exclaimed. Let's see if you can beat that.

Bushy picked up the dice and tumbled them in the palms of his cupped hands and blew on them before expelling them onto the hood where they each stopped on a five. "Double five!" he exclaimed. W.C. issued a mild explicative that dealt with horse excrement and handed Bushy the dollar.

"Slick told me that you stopped to help two guys in a yellow pickup down on the curve Saturday afternoon. Do you remember that?"

"You know I do! I sure wasn't offering those boys any assistance. I'm about a frog hair away from killing both of 'um. I've been waiting for that young'un to draw down on me with that shotgun he carries, but I think the older one holds him back."

"Well, one of them shot at Slick and his buddy earlier that day."

"Hum, if I'd known that I would have broken 'um up and left 'um for the Sheriff."

"The Sheriff wants to talk to them, but he doesn't know who they are or where to find them."

"Now W.C., the older one goes by Red, and the other one is named Danny. I know where they live If that would help. I run by that place two or three times a week."

"Oh, yeah? Where's that?"

"They're about a mile south on the west side of Hagen Road. There's a ramshackle trailer and a little storage shed that sits off the road about 80 yards."

"Thanks!" He thought about the location and expelled a long slow breath. "That's good to know." The sheriff would be glad to know as well, he thought.

And just before he hit the road, Bushy replied, "And W.C., any time you decide to talk to those boys, if you know what I mean, just let me know. Cause I'm ready." And he resumed his jaunt in the gravel and on the warming surface of the blacktop.

13

Slick entered the house through the back door when he came home from school. He hoped to dodge, or at least prolong the exposure of his new shiner. It was already turning dark blue and there were signs of red and purple in the outside corner. But he didn't escape the eye of his mother, who was in the washroom folding laundry. He opened the refrigerator door and searched for a snack, or at least some cover from her watchful eye.

"You better not be drinking from the milk carton." She entered the room and got a glass for him. But he quickly turned and closed the door to make his escape. "Here's a glass," she offered.

"That's okay, Mom," he answered in retreat. But she poured a glass and followed him to his room, where she knocked and entered.

She surprised him as he studied the new fashion statement he sported. "Glen Moore!" she exclaimed. One of the few times she didn't call him Slick. "What on God's green earth has happened to you.?"

"If I told you I picked it up playing basketball at lunch, would you believe me?" He glanced at her with his open right eye and the swelling in his left eye was even more prominent.

"If you say so," she said as she studied the boy behind the eye. "I'm not so sure your father is going to buy that, though," she replied in a doubtful manner and with a questioning face.

He took a deep breath and exhaled. "J.J. hit me."

"My word, J.J. is your best friend!"

"Apparently, not anymore," he spoke as he gestured to his eye.

"But why?

"I think it was all about the portrait of Annie."

She took a slow breath as she covered her mouth softly saying, "Oh, no," as she exhaled. "He was a bit jealous, I guess?"

"I was going to give it to Annie. I wasn't going to show it to the whole class, but Mr. Smith dropped it from my folder when he was showing the skull drawing. That's when J.J. saw it. Everybody saw it. We talked about drawing one of the girls when we were on the river. You know, kinda kiddin' around. I laughed and told him that a girl sure wouldn't like him after she saw his drawing of her. I was just kidding, Mom. And then I saw him wad up a page from his art folder. I didn't know any of this was going to happen."

"He'll get over it soon enough, and everything will be just like it was." She consoled him. "It'll take longer for the eye to heal than it will for J.J. to come around."

"I don't know, Mom. He was really mad, and then Annie took a shine to me and held my hand when we walked down the hall."

"Oh, she did, did she?"

"I wasn't embarrassed, though. I think she felt sorry for me."

"Umm, so that's what you think, huh? Just maybe she's a little sweet on you."

"I don't know, Momma. I've never had a girlfriend before. How will I know?"

"Oh, you'll know. I think you do know!" She smiled and put her hand on his shoulder. "Now let's get some ice on that eye."

With that, she left for the kitchen.

Slick stayed in his room until she called him for dinner. He didn't even come out when W.C. arrived just after five. Ellen had told him the entire story by then and he was prepared to see the bruised eye. Slick wasn't looking forward to the conversation.

"Look who's decided to join the living!" W.C. continued, "I hope you can see the plate all right." W.C.'s joke was met with a frown from Ellen.

"That's enough joking about the eye." There was a sense of finality in her tone. "Boys, say grace please, and let's enjoy the meal."

After everyone had their plates filled with navy beans, fried potatoes and salmon patties, one of the little ones asked, "Does it hurt?"

Slick paused and looked up to see them all staring at him. He shrugged and said, "Not really. Other than the fact that everybody has to see it, it's the best black eye I've ever had."

They all went back to eating. Then the little one said, "I don't want one!"

"It's not so bad if you get what comes with it." And Slick gave him a smile.

"What do you get with it?" he inquired.

"Why, the beautiful princess, of course!"

There was some chuckle at the response, then the little one said, "I don't like girls!"

Everybody laughed. And, W.C. said, "That'll all change someday." And he met Slick's eye with a wink.

14

Buster had been on stakeout until he was relieved at five pm. He was tired, hungry, and out of snuff. He stopped at The Driller and ordered a burger, curly fries and large, sweet tea. His burger was better than a rib-eye steak, he thought. He was as hungry as he'd been in a long time. He had covered his fries and burger with catsup. A little one at the next table watched him with big eyes. When he was done with the catsup, he acted like he was going to squirt the kid with the bottle and laughed. The frightened six-year-old withdrew to his seat and was corrected by his mother. She gave Buster a look of disapproval, thinking his actions were not those of an authority figure. It was, however, true form for Buster. He often acted on impulse. He and the boy continued to exchange looks until they were finished with their meal and left the table. As they went out the door, the kid seized a last-minute opportunity to quickly stick his tongue out at Buster and run before the deputy could retaliate.

He was so busy eating and gaming with the kid that he didn't realize the yellow ford pickup parked beside his unit. Red came inside and picked up a to-go order. Buster was working now. He kept his head down and waited for them to leave, watching where they would go. He would call the sighting in and find out what to do.

When he returned to his unit, he radioed to report the location of the subject vehicle.

"Unit four to unit one, come in, Bob." After a few moments, he tried again. He was tailing the pickup at a distance. "Unit four to unit one, are you there, Bob?"

"What's up, Buster? I've been trying to reach you for thirty minutes. Where have you been?" Bob was noticeably upset.

"I've been eating at the Driller. I just—" and he was interrupted by Bob.

"Buster, did you remember to call in your location?"

"No." He strung out the answer as he thought back, "I guess I was too," and he didn't have the chance to finish before Bob cut in.

"Did you have your hand set off again?" Bob had given him several warnings about calling in and turning his handset on when he was out of the unit.

"Bob, I'm following the yellow pickup. Do you want me to see where it's headed?" He thought the report would help him dodge trouble. But he was wrong.

"No. Do not follow. I repeat, do not follow. I don't want them to know we're watching. I'll just knock on their door," he told him. "W.C. called in their residence earlier today and I have a unit watching nearby. I want to see you in my office at seven sharp in the morning. Do you copy?"

He paused before answering, "Copy," came the reply. He slammed the steering wheel and console of his SUV and reached for the roll of snuff he had purchased at the Quick Stop before going to The Driller. It was gone, and so was his bullet proof vest. He cursed, and then stopped the vehicle to give it a thorough search. They were both gone.

"I don't think he was following us after all. It looks like he pulled over. Maybe he's going to set up a speed trap," Red speculated. "You can ease up, Danny. You're always so tense. You need to learn to relax and act like nothing's the matter." He coached the young accomplice.

"Red," he replied. "I didn't get a chance to show you what I did." He reached behind the seat to the jump seats and pulled out a bullet proof vest. Just like a rabbit from a hat.

"What the—" Red started but Danny interrupted.

"The window was down on the cruiser and the vest was in the seat. It was like it was meant to be, free for the taking. Ya' know what I mean?" Danny hoped he'd understand.

"How can you be sure nobody saw you?"

"They didn't, Red, promise. I looked all around really good! That Deputy screwed up and I was there to clean up!" Then he held up the roll of Copenhagen and started laughing. "And look what else he had. "

15

From where the second deputy sat, he could see that the truck didn't move all night. He had nothing to report on Wednesday morning. But other eyes were closer. Bushy was buried in the trees and early undergrowth near the storage building. He could hear almost everything the men said. They spoke of having a bullet proof vest and moving some product on Saturday. They spent about three hours working in the shed and slept the remainder of the night. He'd tell W.C. first thing in the morning, and he could pass it along to the sheriff.

Wednesday was the last day of school. Students would become kids again. When the final bell rang, the celebration of summer would begin. Slick wasn't so happy as others. He had just met a girl that was more than just a friend, and she would fly to a distant home in France on Saturday. At the Moores', you'd think summer vacation had already begun. All the books were turned in and the little ones had end of school parties. Breakfast was a madhouse. Boxes of cereal and milk flew across the table, and spoons flashed like sabers in an epic final battle. All were anxious for the day to begin. W.C. was already at work and Ellen would serve as hostess at the end of school party for the youngest. The final duty she had as room mother.

"Mom," he said in a somewhat pensive tone. "Do you think it would be okay if I took Annie to the discovery site at the river? She really wants to go, and we get out early today," he asked as he helped clean up after breakfast.

"Today? You want to take her today?" She paused her cleanup, as if she had time. "I really wish you had asked your father, or even earlier, so we could talk it over." He could see her concern and understood. Two young teens, on the river, alone. But this time, one of them was a female.

He assured her that he had no intention other than honorable. "Mom, it's not like we'd do anything bad. I mean, I've never even kissed a girl." And he paused to let her think about it. Then added, "We'll come here after dismissal, and you can talk to us both. Say anything you want. You can call Dad if you need to."

She smiled. "Son," she began, as the little ones blew past them to the car. Already calling out their desired seating position. "Son," she continued, "does she have permission for such a thing as a hike to the river? We don't want any trouble with her host parents."

"They're cool with it. Mom, everybody knows about what we found. They all want to go. But I only want to take her. It's taped off, anyway. We can't get to it." They could hear two short horn blasts from the anxious brothers.

"I will talk to your father. We will expect to see you both here, after school. And, Glen Moore, I expect you to always treat this young lady with utmost respect. Understood?"

"Yes, ma'am! Always!" She picked up her clutch from the counter and the horn blew again. As the door opened, He said, "You look like a million dollars, Mom!" And she did.

When the boys were properly cautioned about the horn, and buckled in for safety, they backed from the drive and headed for the highway. She saw Bushy jogging toward the intersection, and they all waved. Such a nice man with a strange habit. She called W.C. and told him about Slick wanting to take Annie to the river. He told her that he trusted Slick to do what was proper, and she told him that it wasn't Slick that she was worried about. He laughed, and she told him that she saw Bushy jogging toward the house when she left. "I'll check that out, hon, and don't worry about Slick. Go and have fun at the party!" She could feel him smiling at the thought of twenty-two kiddos celebrating the last day of school. "I'll check on Bushy."

It took W.C. ten minutes to make it to the house where he found Bushy sitting on the front porch. He was dressed in camo print pants and had green and black face paint on his upper body. Slick had already caught his ride to school. Bushy went to greet W.C. as he pulled into the drive. He placed his carbine across the hood of the truck just as always. "My turn to roll first, ain't it?" he remembered.

"Yup." And W.C. pulled out the dice. Just like always, Bushy cupped the dice in his hands and blew some luck on them. When they spilled out onto the hood, box cars were facing up.

"Yee-Haw!" he exclaimed. "You can try to match that if you think you're lucky," he said.

"You lucky little turd! Give me those bones." He rubbed them in his flattened hands and bumped them off the forehand stock of the rifle. "Snake eyes!" he uttered dejectedly. W.C. pulled a dollar from his wallet and paid his debt. Then he said, "Let's try one more time."

They never rolled twice unless it was double or nothing. W.C. laid a crisp hundred on the hood and the mild breeze pushed it up by the trigger guard of the rifle. Before he saw it stop moving, Bushy had one in his hand and was about to put it down. "Wait a minute here!" He scooped the hundred up quicker than catching a fly. "I was just bluffing, Bushy."

"I thought maybe you grabbed the wrong bill by mistake," he said with whimsical overtones and a big smile and a chuckle.

"There's no way I'm rollin' the dice against you again today. And, dang sure not for a hundred of my dollars."

"You're smart, W.C.. But anytime you're ready, just pull that big 'un out again."

W.C. jutted his chin and raised one brow while shaking his head. "Now, what's got you here at the house this early in the day?"

"Well, Mr. Moore. Last night, I bellied up to the shed down at the end of Hagen Road."

"Are you saying you sneaked in at their place? I wondered why you were dressed this way." He was alarmed.

"Just a little recon mission. I had my ear against the building, listening. Bob is gonna want to know what they're doing," he said and waited for a reply.

"I guess they're cooking meth. Right?"

"Yeah, but they're gonna deliver the finished product on Saturday. And that's not all. They took a bullet proof vest from one of the deputies. The sheriff probably knows that by now."

"Did they say where they were delivering the stuff or who they were meeting?"

"Nope. And you can tell Bob that his deputy is too easy to spot and I'm sure he didn't see a thing."

"Maybe, but I don't want you anywhere near those boys. That means no more recon." He emphasized the last statement by raising his voice. "Somebody's gonna get hurt before this business is done. Let's give 'um some space and let Bob take care of it. Okay?"

"Understood, sir." He snapped to attention, saluted and then smiled before he picked up his weapon and jogged away.

Because of recent developments, W.C. had Bob's cell on speed dial. It's not every parent that can say that. He answered after the third ring.

"W.C. Moore," he answered in a matter-of-fact tone. "What can I do for you today?"

"I've got some news about our druggies in the yellow pickup."

"What you got?" he inquired.

"I have it on authority," and he paused. "That they will make a delivery of finished goods on Saturday."

"What authority?" He wanted to know, since he should be the authority.

"I don't want to get anybody in trouble," W.C. said. "But I'd stake a hundred on it being the truth." And he almost did.

"W.C., if you know somebody that's on the inside, you need to tell me."

"I know. I just don't want to get 'um in trouble."

"It's that jogger, isn't it? He's the one that told you where they lived. I'll just pick him up and question him myself."

"Bob, I don't think that's a good idea. He'll go so far underground you'll never find him."

"I have cause, you know. Running the road with that rifle."

"He's never fired it, Bob. Not once. But he knows how. It's no different than me carryin' my rifle in the truck. Is it?"

And the sheriff paused before he answered. "I guess not, W.C. I don't want him mixed up in this. It could get a little sticky if you know what I mean."

"I've told him to stand down and I think he understands. But there's more."

"Okay, let's have it." He felt like he was on the outside looking in.

"He heard them talking about having a bullet-proof-vest they took from one of your deputies."

Bob blew a gasket. "Somebody, find Buster, and get him back in here!" The man was livid. The desk deputy immediately dropped her folder and began radioing the deputy. He couldn't be that far away. Bob had just finished giving the deputy a forty-five-minute butt-chewing. This one was gonna be bad!

W.C. heard Bob blow up. Even with his hand over the phone. "Thanks, W.C.. Stay in touch. Okay?"

"You bet, Bob."

16

The two walked to the bus hand in hand. Annie was anxious to see the skeleton and Slick wondered if anything had been done at the site since he was there on Sunday. It was a fifteen-minute ride to the house by bus. They were the oldest riders, and the bus was mostly empty. Many were picked up by parents on the last day of school. The driver eased the bus to a stop and opened the door.

"Slick, you kids have a good summer, and try to stay out of trouble." The driver issued his last goodbye for the summer.

"Thanks, Artie. Have a good summer, too. I know you've earned it." He smiled at the thought of a summer on the lake.

They could hear the door shut behind them and the boys were chasing one another around the house with squirt guns. A gift they received at the end of year party. A crude joke by the principal who was no doubt laughing at his desk at this very moment.

"Don't you dare squirt us with those guns." They seemed to heed the warning as they dropped their hands.

The little one studied the visitor and asked, "Is this the beautiful princess?" Annie blushed.

"Doesn't she look like one?" Slick asked.

Then staring at the visitor, he said, "Yep! I like her!" He immediately turned to the other one and raised his pistol for a shot in the face. The chase continued.

"Come on in and I'll introduce you to Mom."

As they walked to the door, she said, "Did you tell them I was a beautiful princess?"

"Well, yes. Is that okay?"

"I'm quite flattered, actually. A girl needs to feel like a beautiful princess now and again. I'm very happy that you told them that."

He helped her up the steps and opened the door just as he had seen W.C. do for his mom. His dad was a fine example of a gentleman.

Ellen heard them and entered the room, very much like a princess herself. She had a rough morning wrestling the entire class. It was trying. She had taken the time to freshen up her appearance after she got home. She wanted to make a good first impression.

"Annie, this is my mom, Mrs. Ellen Moore. Mom this is Annie." Annie extended her hand and made a slight curtsey, showing her French up-bringing.

"It's a pleasure to meet you, Mrs. Moore. You're so beautiful and have such a nice home and family. I wish we had the opportunity to meet sooner."

"Why, thank you, Annie. I'm so glad Slick has met such a polite young lady."

"Jake already asked her if she was the beautiful princess."

"Oh, I'm so sorry." And then chuckled.

He said, "I like her."

"That's quite a statement coming from the boy who has sworn to hate girls," Ellen said. "Please have a seat and I'll get you something to drink. Would you like a glass of water or soft drink?"

"I love cola, if you have it," Annie responded.

"One cola, coming up." And she seemed to float to the kitchen.

They spoke of family and school and her Saturday flight home, pausing only for an occasional water gun refill for the boys.

Buster was waiting at the end of Hagen Road. He no longer wore the uniform of a deputy. In a somewhat warranted and much heated discussion, Bob dismissed him from his position. That's a polite way of saying he was fired. But after he left the sheriff's office and before he was recalled, he picked up the word that the drug runners lived at the end of Hagen Road. He wanted to confront them about the vest, his job, and a thirty-six-dollar roll of snuff. The deputy on stakeout knew nothing of Buster's termination and was easily convinced that he was working the case from the inside.

17

W.C. arrived home about three o'clock and met the young lady visitor. She treated him with the same pleasantries that she had displayed for Ellen. He was impressed with how she handled herself. And he even got a thumbs up from Jake on the way inside, not to mention a good spray with the squirt guns. He carried a package in his left hand. Shortly after meeting Annie, he tossed the package to Slick.

"This has been a long time coming, son. It'll help us stay in touch."

Slick opened the sack and found a new iPhone. "I told you we would talk about it. But with everything going on lately, I thought it would be a good idea to go ahead and get it. The number is on the sack."

"Thanks, Dad."

"You two better get on the road if you're planning on getting any exploring done," and he nodded toward the door. "Remember son…be respectful!"

They headed in a direct line to the river. She had packed a small fanny pack with two apples and a bottle of water.

"Will it take long to get there?" she asked.

"It's about a twenty-minute walk. We'll be there before you know it," he told her.

She reached to hold his hand for no reason other than it felt right. She had been accepted by his family and trusted to be respectful and respected in return.

"Listen to the breeze," he told her. "Listen away from us as it makes its way along the grass and through the fence ahead. Can you hear it?"

"Yes," she said, after pausing just a moment.

"Now, listen as it moves past your hair, you're clothing and your ears. Can you hear that, too?"

"Yes, Slick. I hear it," replying more quickly than before.

"Now listen to them at the same time. That's the very breath of Mother Nature, whispering to us. Isn't it great?"

"It's wonderful! I've never really paid close attention before."

"Just wait until we make it to the river. You'll be on sound overload. There's so much to hear and it all competes for the chance to be heard."

Later, as they approached the river, he stopped. "Listen to the leaves rustle in the trees, each one singing its own song, trying to be heard above the others. They're like thousands upon thousands of people in a stadium. Waving and shouting and touching each other. People are very much a part of nature. Don't you think?"

"I have never thought about it. I didn't know you were such a naturalist." And then she took time to listen and think before responding, "Like Thoreau?"

"That guy's out of my league, I like nature, but I'm not a transcendentalist. Those guys were too far out there for me. I'm not a philosopher. I just love nature."

"It's a surprise that you have read of such things."

"We do have library books, you know," and he smiled at her. He stopped again as they approached the gulley. "Listen to the birds." The blackbirds were feeding in the field and moving in waves to the field ahead of the others. The woodpecker was tapping a tree in search of his next meal. And quail were calling their name, 'Bob White'.

"They are beautiful, Slick. This is the place, I guess?" She waited for him to lead her by the hand so she could peer at the skeleton.

"Here, now look into the gully, suspended in the wall. Do you see it?" and he looked into her face. She was fearful, yet brave.

"It's such a strange thing, you know, to see someone like that." She held him closely.

"He's probably been buried there for over three-hundred-fifty years. Maybe more. That's my guess. But I'm not an anthropologist, either. They'll do all kinds of testing to date him. I was just going by the coins."

"How did he come to be at this place? I just wonder."

"Best guess is that he was an explorer. Maybe he was with Coronado and was separated from the others. Maybe he was killed by Indians. I choose to think he decided to live here. Like me. And he died of old age. But he wasn't alone. Someone buried him and placed coins over his eyes."

"Why do such a thing? It seems like such a waste of money."

"Well, I know what you mean, but what was he going to spend it on? There were no stores or markets. Someone thought it was a worthy use of the coins to pay the ferryman for passage to the underworld."

"This is a real thing. This ferryman." Her eyes were almost as big as the Spanish dollars.

"No, I don't believe so. But many, many non-Christians did years ago. That's what Mr. Smith told me. I'd never heard of it before."

"What will become of it? I mean, him?" She searched for the proper term.

"I suspect the authorities will fight over him until they decide who he belongs to. The State and Federal Indian authorities will have first shot after the coroner. I can see they have taken a lower leg that was in the bottom of the gulley."

"Oh no! Will they bring it back?"

"I hope so. I just want them to look for answers and cover him back up. Enough about him. Let's go down to the spring." Hand in hand they made their way down the riverbank. It seemed like the stones were cobbled for easy passage. He didn't remember them being that way. There had been other visitors to the spring. The coroner and other officials had no doubt followed the sound of the spring and river. He was pleased they had left it pristine.

"What is all this? It falls from the big tree." She stooped to gather a big handful of cottonwood seed.

"That's the seed of the cottonwood tree. Look up at the big clusters still hanging on the branches. It's in full bloom now. I don't remember seeing one like this before. See the little clusters that haven't ruptured. Those are called catkins. That's how the tree reproduces."

While he was staring in the tree and teaching biology, she had amassed a handful of the fluffy white seeds and when he turned to see her, she stood and threw them in his face. "Got you, Slick Moore!"

Brushing the seed from his face, "I reckon you did!" A snowball fight, in June with a pretty girl. I guess it doesn't get any better than this. They had a brief exchange of gathered and pressed puffs of seed that were hurriedly thrown at each other. They laughed and the tension Annie felt while gazing at the remains seemed to float away with the little seeds. Some flew away with the breeze and others followed the gurgle and tumble of the spring water, where they entered the river traveling to who knows where.

"Come on and we'll look for arrow heads." She followed him to the mouth of the stream where she opened the fanny pack and took a drink of water. She offered him a drink, but he shook his head no.

"I've got water. All I can drink." He moved back up the stream and fell to his knees, filling his cupped hands with water. It was cool, clear and refreshing.

"Glen Moore!" She sounded like his mother. "You will surely become ill with only me to nurse you."

"Annie, I'm not gonna get sick," reassuring her he would be okay. "Me and J.J. must have drunk a half-gallon each just four days ago. And do I look ill? Come on and take a sip."

She studied him briefly and thought how courageous he was to drink from the untamed waters of the spring. "I believe I'll just finish the bottle. It will be enough, thank you."

"Okay, suit yourself. I respect your choice. Now let's look for arrowheads." He removed his shoes and socks and raised the legs of his jeans. Annie followed his example. He stepped into the convergence of the waters and extended his hand. She let him help her into the refreshing chill of the ankle-deep mixture.

"It's nice, isn't it? Better than a bathtub or swimming pool." He tried to convince her.

"I think I do like it. I didn't think I would," and she moved her foot around in the water. "But I do! It's relaxing," she said as she looked into his eyes.

He broke away from those big brown eyes and demonstrated how to search for arrowheads. "Like this." He demonstrated the method he and J.J. had perfected before. "I should have brought Mom's garden trowel. She wouldn't have cared." They had minimal success only finding broken fragments from a failed attempt to make a weapon.

"I need something to dig with." She was working vigorously in one spot.

"Let me see what you've found." And he took out his pocketknife and started to dig.

"No," she stopped him with a gentle touch to his arm and held the other hand out for the knife. "Let me, please. I want to find this myself."

"Okay, but carefully." He held the knife until she melted his stern look with those warm brown eyes. "You know, if you hurt yourself, you'll be stuck with me to patch you up," paraphrasing her earlier statement.

"Glen, mon amie," she said with a smile. "You must trust me." He offered the knife with the blade open.

It was the first time she had spoken his name in a French statement. It made him feel warm inside. Closer to her in some way. She began gouging and digging with the knife, using both hands. She dug with the knife in her right hand and used her left to move the object around until it came free.

"Look at this! I have found something good, yes!" she was rapidly rinsing and rubbing the best specimen of a lance point you could ever hope to find. It was perfectly preserved in a point down position. It was still very sharp, and she cut her finger as she rushed to clean it in the cool spring water. He put the knife away and took her injured hand.

"Let me see, mon amie," he said using her words. Besides, it sounded a little cute, he thought.

"Do you know what it is that you say?"

He shook his head. "No." Which was the truth and he continued to clean her hand.

"Let me teach you some French. Oui?" and he nodded yes. "Oui, means yes, or I agree. Would you like to learn one more thing?"

"Oui," he said with confidence.

She squeezed his hand and said, "Mon amie means friend. If you say, mon amie Annie, it means my friend, Annie. But if you say, Annie mon amie, it means Annie, my girlfriend. Oui?"

He thought about it, and said, "Oui, Annie, mon amie." And he gently kissed her injured finger before helping her from the water.

Together, they inspected the lance point. It would have been a threatening weapon on the end of an eight-foot pole. A lance had obviously been thrust into the area that was the mouth of the stream. Perhaps as a marker of some sort that stood for good water, or maybe denoted tribal property. Maybe it marked a stop on a cross continental trade route. Traders would swap chert to make arrowheads for tanned hides and dried venison. Time and rising water had separated the shaft from the buried stone point. "You've got yourself a keeper, Annie."

"Yes, very nice." She placed it in the fanny pack for safe keeping. And she pulled out an apple and offered it to him.

"Good idea. We'll eat the apples and start home. It has been a good day, oui?"

"Oui, Slick, mon amie." He was beginning to like the sound of that. And he really liked the look on her face when she said it.

They sat with their feet in the water and began to eat the apples. Eating an apple was a slow and sensual process for Annie. He could hardly eat a bite watching her. She would take a small bite and slowly chew, then swallow. She frequently moistened her lips with her tongue. Like the head of a small serpent, it parted her lips and moistened them completely. Then, she would press her lips together like he'd seen women do after using lipstick or gloss. He watched her eat the entire apple. And I mean the entire apple. She was very aware of him watching, but it was not a performance. When she got to the core, she held it by the stem and ate it in two bites.

He was intrigued by the site. The thought of it would have been strange enough. Watching it happen was the next level. So, he asked, "Do you always eat the core of the apple?"

Pausing and moistening her lips again, she said, "It is only more apple to me. Oui?" And then she looked him in the eye and winked as she put the stem between her teeth and began to chew and swallow it. Then she moistened her lips once more as he watched and puckered up like she was giving him a kiss. Perhaps she would have, but Chasity made an appearance at the top of the trail.

18

When Red and Danny were approaching their trailer after work, they saw a light blue step side chevy pickup parked at the end of the road. The hood was up like there was a malfunction of some kind. Red was very leery of any vehicle at the end of Hagen Road because there was nothing but their trailer and their shed at the end of the road.

"I wonder what this is all about. Danny, you just stay put and I'll check it out." He moved cautiously toward the truck and called out, "Hello. Anybody there?" He walked up to the truck and called again, "Do you need help?" He could see no one in the vicinity. So, he checked the cab of the truck. The keys were in the ignition and the console had a driver license and registration for Buster Reid. By then Danny was at his side. "I told you to stay put!" Danny was looking over his shoulder.

"Hey, that's the deputy that left the window down over at The Driller. What's he doing here? He looked around. Then asked. "Where is he anyway?"

"I don't like the looks of this, Danny. Get your gun and let's look around. I'll try the trailer first." He cautiously approached the trailer and climbed up the steps of the rickety porch. There was no way to be quiet. The aging boards creaked under his weight, announcing his approach. He did a room-to-room search and found nothing unusual. Nothing missing and nothing out of place. No sign of entry. And the deputy's vest was still on the small dining table. Red stepped back outside and tossed the vest to Danny. "Here, put this on." He scurried to put it on, but it wasn't adjusted properly. Buster was more rotund than Danny. Red watched him, keeping an eye on the surrounding area. "That's good enough. Now let's check the shed."

The shed was really an old metal and wood structure that had been used as a garage for over sixty years. At some point, double doors were added to the large opening on the south side. It was the only entrance. And it had been used. Two sets of footprints had entered the makeshift drug lab. One set had the print of a popular name brand sneaker that was worn by men of all ages. The other bore the tread of a common tire you could find on half the cars in the county. But not in the shape of a man's size ten. Red saw the markings and motioned for Danny to be ready. Without a sound, he held up three fingers and mimed 'on three'. Then he motioned the count with his left hand. Simultaneously, they blew through the doors like a hard spring thunderstorm but found no one.

"We had two visitors, Danny."

"I saw the tracks." And he quickly added, "One of 'um was that Indian boy."

"Keep your voice down. We don't know where they are. Looks like he's teamed up with the law."

Danny made a face. "That Deputy? I ain't afraid of him." Then quickly added, "I ain't afraid of that road runnin' Indian either. And then he tapped the vest with his index finger.

Red was listening more to the outside world than to Danny but turned his head toward him and spoke, "I've been telling you to cool it about that guy. Now listen to me. I went into the shop this morning to get two tubes of grease for the machine. I asked the mechanic about him, and Gene said, 'not to bother him'. He's a decorated war hero, Danny. He's dodged bullets in the sands of the middle east and the jungles of Central America. He saved the lives of every soldier in his unit, by capturing a machine gun post and using it against them. He didn't take any prisoners, Danny." He was slowly shaking his head no.

"I'm not afraid of him! See this!" He grabbed the loosely fitted vest with his left hand and pulled it away from his body.

Red pressed his pistol hard into Danny's nose. "How do you think the vest'll do against a bullet right here?" He held the muzzle against him for three seconds, and then pushed him back with it. "To top that off, you'll never see it coming." He turned his attention to the north-east corner of the shed where there was a waist high stack of lumber. He began to throw it to either side until he found his stash. "It looks like it's all here! Let me see." He counted the bundles of money and plastic wrapped bricks of crystal meth. "It's here. All of it. That's the only thing that's been good about this day. That and a new truck."

"Are we taking the deputy's truck?"

"No, Danny! We're gonna wait till he comes back and offers to give him some drug money for it. Don't you think he'll go along with that?"

"No," and he stared at Red. "I ain't dumb as you think." He paused to give Red a little time to answer. Then hearing nothing he continued, "I'm smart enough to know we gotta go! We can't wait here anymore. I saw you count out three hundred fifty thousand dollars. There's at least another four hundred thousand in those bundles of drugs. We've gotta go while we can."

"You're right. We've gotta go." After a brief pause, he stuffed the cash and drugs into an athletic bag. It was so full it wouldn't zip. "You go ahead and check to see that it's clear." He paused long enough to look at him and said, "And Danny, why don't you clean out anything from the truck that we don't want to leave behind."

"You bet, Red!" He left with a new energy. Finally, he felt like an equal part of the operation.

Red was close behind. As soon as Danny entered the truck on the passenger side where he had logged thousands of miles, Red called his name. "Danny?" It was like a question. But when he turned, Red leveled his automatic at his face. "Sorry, Buddy." He pulled the trigger. It would be easier to be on the run alone. He had never killed anyone before. It was Danny that always wanted to pull the trigger on somebody. He was saddened by the sudden end to their relationship but had no time to reflect. He covered the interior of the truck and the engine with gasoline. He emptied the remainder of the five gallons of fuel on the garage wall and turned the gas on in the trailer. He barely got Buster's truck started before everything was involved in flames.

He drove toward the intersection and looked in the rearview only one time. "I'm sorry Danny. Real Sorry."

Buster never knew what happened. He turned his truck around at the trailer and found no one at home. He was going to plead his case with the men. He wanted his vest and job back. At least he would maybe get his respect back. He enjoyed the way people treated him as a deputy, and now he had lost that. As soon as he had tried to open the doors to the garage, he was jumped from behind. Bushy was quick and quiet. He knew what would happen if he was caught no matter what his intent. And now, he would be in danger as well. His tracks were definite whether barefoot or sandaled. But he couldn't allow Buster to get himself killed. Bushy carried him out through the mesquites to the west and turned back north hoping to hit the road to Cook's Corner. He heard the muffled sound of a single gunshot and saw the smoke from the trailer at the end of Hagen Road. He could have predicted that. Nothing covers tracks like fire. This also meant that the drugs were in the vehicle. Bushy was now running down the highway with Buster on his back.

"Stop. Hey, what are you doing? Put me down!" He didn't ask who. That was obvious.

"Okay, but you've gotta promise not to run away. We stay together. Deal?" Bushy insisted.

"What if I don't wa—" He didn't finish the statement before being interrupted.

"I'll let you take another nap and carry you to my lair like a wild animal." Bushy was a convincing character and he looked like he could carry out the threat.

"Just jog with me for a while." The deputy is about a hundred yards up the road. "I'll let you go when we get there. Promise. And you're welcome, by the way."

"For what?" He hadn't a clue.

"I just saved your worthless tail, that's what." He motioned to the plume of smoke rising into the sky as the stench of the smoke had made it to the highway. It was a smell Bushy was familiar with. "That's the smell of burning flesh."

19

"Don't be afraid, it's just Chasity." Slick reassured Annie. "She lives here. Well, all around here I guess."

The big dog was waiting to be introduced and moved slowly to Annie.

"This is Annie. She's my girl." And he glanced at Annie. "Hold your hand out like this." He held his hand toward the gentle giant, and she licked it like she was trying to clean up from the apple he had already finished. "See, she's a lover. Just a big pet. Go on, let her smell your hand." Annie curtsied and held her hand toward Chasity like a formal greeting. She smelled Annie's hand and then her face. First, Annie was frozen in place, with the big dog's head only inches away. Then she began to laugh as Chasity licked her face.

"Darn it, Chasity!" he exclaimed. "You're kissin' my girl before I even have the chance to kiss her myself!" Annie held the dog's massive head with both hands and let those dark eyes do their magic as she burned a hole into Slick's heart.

"But Glen, Mon Amie. You silly boy! Have you offered to kiss? I have been waiting for you." She released her hold on Chasity, and the big pup looked at him and tilted her head like she wanted an answer herself. "Have you never kissed a girl?" she asked.

He was slow to answer, then replied, "No," and he paused just for a moment. "But I think I'm ready." They moved toward each other and met in an embrace that turned into their first kiss. It proved to be sweet, memorable and shorter than they wanted, as Slick's new phone rang for the first time. His dad's number was on the screen.

"Hello, Dad. What's up?"

"Hey, Slick. Ya'll having fun?" His opening was slow. But he hated to start with a threatening statement in the first sentence of his first call.

"Yeah, Dad. You're not going to believe the neat spear tip Annie found." She could hear both sides of the conversation.

"Listen to me, son. I just picked up Bushy and Buster on the highway west of Hagen Road. At least one of the men from the river has taken Buster's truck and he's on the run. I'm headed your way. Just stay put. I'll come and pick you both up. Do you understand?" Annie was scared listening to W.C. She could tell he was worried. So, she was afraid.

"Yes, Dad. Is that what the sirens are all about?" They could hear them over the phone as W.C. met the Fire Department on the way to the fire.

"There's a fire close-by us, but don't be surprised if you hear more sirens. They're tryin' to set up roadblocks and stop him. I talked to Bob and he and a deputy got on it pretty quick."

The hikers could hear faint sirens now. They stopped about a mile east of them where they were putting out nail strips and blocking the road. "We can hear the sirens to the east, Dad. Is he coming this way?" He needed to know.

"There's just three ways out of town, son. The authorities have them blocked and I'm coming to you! Stay put! Is that clear." He was using his matter-of-fact Dad voice.

"Yes, sir." What else can you say to a statement like that.

"Just stay on the phone and keep out of sight until you see me driving up. Is Annie okay? Is she afraid? You guys are having a first date to remember for a long, long time."

"You have no idea!" Annie smiled. "She's cool, Dad. She smiled at your comments."

"Son, I'm headed your way and I can see him in front of me. There's a State Trooper between us, and he's closing fast."

"We can hear the siren getting louder."

"They just made the curve. He sees the roadblock and he's turning around." His voice was getting louder and faster like a sports announcer calling a goal at a soccer game. "He's headed back toward us." Slick could hear Bushy saying how he wishes he had his rifle and Buster made a comment about how he might have a bullet proof vest. "Oh, my!" W.C. yelled out. He could hear the other men yelling too, but couldn't make out what they were saying, like they were in the announcer's booth as well. "He kept going west at the curve and ran through the fence in the back! He's on foot, Slick! He's on foot and he's headed your way carrying a bag of some kind. Slick, it's the guy with the green cap! Can you hear me?

"We're staying here like you said! Are you coming?"

"I can't see him anymore, but I know he's headed your way."

"Hurry, Dad! Just hurry!

"We're coming through the gate right now!

Red was headed northwest and was hoping to use the river for cover and slip away during the night. Before he made it to the field where the gully was, he stepped on a very large rattler. When he was bitten, he jumped and landed on yet another rattler and was bitten a second time. He fired his gun at the snakes and kept moving toward the river.

"Dad, he's shootin'. You hear it?"

"Yes, and I see him runnin' toward you!"

Then, Red began to stumble and fell hard. He picked himself up and tried to re-pack his bag. Money and drugs scattered when he fell. He could pick it up as it was still in bundles. But the snakes' venom was working on him. All that running had pumped it throughout his body. He became disoriented and could only make out the yellow tape around the gully. It was like a beacon. He stumbled toward it.

Slick and Annie were holding Chasity down in the grass at the edge of the bank. They could see W.C. stop and point his rifle out the window the way he always did shooting coyotes.

"This is Bushy! Your dad said to keep your heads down. He ain't gonna let 'em git to ya'."

There was a Trooper pulling beside them and hollering on his speaker. "DO NOT SHOOT! LOWER THE WEAPON!" Of course, he didn't know the teens were only a few steps away. The two cars were sharing info and Bushy was now outside the truck and making tracks toward Red. Red could see them. He heard the speaker on the Trooper's car, and he saw Bushy running straight at him. He could hardly see from the sweat and the venom that blurred his vision, but he aimed to shoot and mumbled, "Danny, this is for you." The first round was errant, but it didn't slow Bushy down. And the second met with interference from Chasity. She broke away from the kids at the sound of the first shot. They could see his face when he turned and saw the three of them. Chasity jumped up and put her big paws on his shoulders. They were face to face and the combination of all the events caused Red to fall into the gully.

Bushy was there first and peered into the gully without any care for his own safety. Red no longer held the automatic and he crumpled headfirst alongside the remains of the explorer. "You kids, okay?"

"Yes, sir! We're sure glad to see ya'll. Where's the other one of them?"

"I'm not sure, but I don't think he made it!"

W.C. and the Trooper pulled up and they could hear the familiar voice of the concerned parent. "Oh my God, Slick! Are you both all right? There for a minute I was pretty scared."

"We're all good, Mr. Moore," Annie answered in a somewhat composed voice, considering. "They're never going to believe this at home!"

The Trooper took his hand off his weapon and snapped it securely in place. "Fella, I've seen some things in my day, but—" and he was gone. Bushy was already thirty yards away, running home. "Strange," was all he said.

"I must say, he is fearless. If you need him, I'll see him tomorrow. I think I owe him a hundred dollars."

20

Mitch locked the gate on the road to the river. There were many people wanting to see the spot where the skeleton was discovered, and he couldn't be responsible if somebody was hurt. He said the boys could still fish any time they wanted so long as he was invited to eat fried fish now and then. The two boys made up after Annie returned home. And, just like his mother said, Slick still had the remains of a black eye the first time they went fishing. They fished at the spring's mouth with success. Ellen fried their catch as soon as they were cleaned, which was her promise from the first fish he ever caught. They had to be careful not to catch more than they could carry. It was a challenge. They always wanted to catch another, maybe bigger fish.

A native sandstone marker was placed at the site where the skeleton was found. It was inscribed, 'Agua de Vida' and below that was 'Water of Life.' Historians had determined that it was the remains of a Spanish explorer and dated the stone rather exactly. "Discovered circa. 1550 A.D." While the Spaniard had found no gold, he stopped at the spring on the Wichita River, and never left. Maybe the discovery of the 'Agua de Vida' or 'Water of Life' was better than gold.